STOLEN TREASURE

THE UNOFFICIAL MINECRAFT MYSTERIES SERIES

BOOK ONE

STOLEN TREASURE

THE UNOFFICIAL MINECRAFT MYSTERIES SERIES

BOOK ONE

Winter Morgan

Sky Pony Press
New York

Copyright © 2018 by Hollan Publishing, Inc.

Minecraft® is a registered trademark of Notch Development AB.

The Minecraft game is copyright © Mojang AB.

Sky Pony Press books may be purchased in bulk at special discounts for sales promotion, corporate gifts, fund-raising, or educational purposes. Special editions can also be created to specifications. For details, contact the Special Sales Department, Sky Pony Press, 307 West 36th Street, 11th Floor, New York, NY 10018 or info@skyhorsepublishing.com.

Sky Pony® is a registered trademark of Skyhorse Publishing, Inc.®, a Delaware corporation.

Minecraft® is a registered trademark of Notch Development AB. The Minecraft game is copyright © Mojang AB.

Visit our website at www.skyponypress.com.

10 9 8 7 6 5 4 3 2 1

Library of Congress Cataloging-in-Publication Data is available on file.

Cover design by Brian Peterson
Cover image by Megan Miller

Print ISBN: 978-1-5107-3187-5
Ebook ISBN: 978-1-5107-3193-6

Printed in Canada

TABLE OF CONTENTS

STOLEN TREASURE

TREASURE IN THE NETHER

"**W**atch out!" Billy called to his friend Edison. "What? Where?" Edison was confused. He wasn't sure which direction he should turn. He looked to the left, but there was only an empty staircase with a patch of soul sand and Nether wart growing on the side.

"Look to the right!" cried Billy. He pulled out his diamond sword and his blue helmet almost fell off his head. He brushed his black hair from his eyes.

From the corner of his eye, Edison could see a dark skeleton sprinting in his direction. Before Edison had time to move, the skeleton plunged his stone sword into Edison's unarmored leg. "Ouch!" he wailed as he was afflicted with the Wither effect, which turned his health bar black and left him frozen and exhausted as he stood powerless in the Nether fortress.

1

Billy slammed his sword into the wither skeleton, but it was a tricky and powerful mob. The skeleton leapt at Billy, striking his arm and unleashing the Wither effect. Billy's voice was low and Edison could barely make out the words that fell from his lips: "We need milk. Do you have any?"

The Wither effect was fading, and Edison mustered up enough energy to reach into his inventory and pull out a bottle and take a sip of milk, instantly energizing him and erasing the damage from the wither skeleton's stone sword. With renewed energy, he grabbed his diamond sword to pierce the skeleton with one hand and handed the milk to Billy with the other. The wither skeleton was destroyed, dropping a skull on the ground that Edison pocketed. Edison felt invigorated, like he could do anything. He had just decimated his first wither skeleton and he'd helped his friend Billy, the legendary treasure hunter.

"Thanks! The milk hit the spot," said Billy. "We have to go down this hall and get the treasure." Billy pointed to a hall beyond the pillar. "But first, you should try and get some soul sand and Nether wart—they're vital for brewing potions, right?"

Edison's brewing supplies were quite low, which was the reason he had accompanied his friend and neighbor on this treasure hunt to the Nether. The morning before, he was working on some new potions at his brewing table, but he was low on so many ingredients that he couldn't brew anything. Both soul sand and Nether wart were essential for making potions, and

Edison knew he had to get as much as he could. He picked a shovel from his inventory and started to collect the soul sand and Nether wart.

"I'll help you." Billy clutched his shovel as he kept an eye out for any other hostile mobs that might be spawning in the dimly lit Nether fortress.

As Edison filled his inventory with the two ingredients, he looked up. "I see a light." There was sliver of light in the distance. "Do you think someone is there?"

"No," Billy replied, "it looks like there is just glowstone on the walls."

"Glowstone?" Edison asked. "Awesome. We can collect glowstone dust. Do we have time to mine a few pieces from the wall?"

"Yes," Billy said, "but we should make it quick because I want to get to the treasure. You never know who is lurking down here, and I want to get to the treasure before anyone else."

"Anyone else?" Edison was confused.

"You never know who is going to show up in the Nether," said Billy.

"I haven't seen anyone down here at all," remarked Edison as he pulled the final bits of Nether wart from the side of the stairs and walked toward the glowing hallway. The Nether fortress was hot, and Edison's brown hair was dripping with sweat. Walking down the hallway, he soaked in the beauty of the luminous wall. He pulled out a pickaxe and broke off a piece of the glowstone and placed it in his inventory.

"I don't need too much. Do you want any?" asked Edison.

Billy shook his head. "I'm fine. I just want to get to this treasure. I think it's down here."

The two walked down the hallway but stopped when they heard a bouncing noise.

"What's that sound?" Edison asked as he nervously took out his diamond sword.

"Magma cubes." Billy pointed to the room in front of them. "We have to destroy them."

"Where are they?" asked Edison. He wasn't a skilled treasure hunter. Despite calling himself an explorer, he hadn't really spent much time in the Nether. He wasn't a fan of the hot, timeless biome where fiery mobs flew through the air and threatened you with fireballs. He much preferred the Overworld, where he'd happily travel through any biome, including the ice and the desert. He understood the Overworld. There was a sense of time. In the Nether, he always felt out of sorts and could never enjoy himself.

"Over here!" Billy hollered as he ripped into a large bouncing magma cube, slicing it into three smaller cubes that surrounded him.

Edison raced to his friend's side, plunging his diamond sword into dark, boxy cubes with piercing, yellow-and-red eyes until they all disappeared.

"Pick up the magma cream," said Billy.

Edison knew magma cream was incredibly helpful when brewing Fire Resistance potions, so he collected it while Billy ran ahead.

"Down here!" Billy called to his friend. "I found it!"

"The treasure?"

"Yes," Billy said. "I'm in the room at the end of the hall."

Edison raced down the hall. As he walked into the room, he saw Billy leaning over an open chest.

"What's in it?" asked Edison.

"Diamonds." Billy showed him the open chest. "Let's split up the loot."

"I see another chest." Edison bolted to the corner and opened a second chest that was filled with iron ingots. "This one's got good loot, too."

"Yeah, I want to check out the other rooms before we leave. Since none of these chests have been emptied, it's a good sign that we might be the first people in this fortress. I'm hoping we find some more treasure."

Edison stuffed his inventory with the contents of the chest, dividing the loot equally between the two of them. When they entered the next room, there was one chest. Billy opened it. "More Nether wart. You can have it all. I don't really use it."

"Seriously?" asked Edison.

"You can pay me back by brewing a potion for me," suggested Billy.

"Deal." Edison emptied the chest of Nether wart, and the duo went off to explore the rest of the Nether fortress.

After perusing each room, they declared the fortress empty. They were ready to exit and craft a portal back to the Overworld when a yellow blaze rose from the ground and shot a fireball at them. Edison quickly grabbed a snowball from his inventory and dodged the flying flame as the cold snowball destroyed the heated mob. Edison reached for the blaze rod that was his reward. "This will come in very handy when I brew potions later today."

"Come on," said Billy, "we should make our way to the portal now. We don't want to arrive in town in the middle of the night. It will make us incredibly vulnerable."

The duo raced from the fortress, but once they stepped outside, they saw three ghasts circling in the sky to guard the fortress. One of the white mobs floated right in front of them, unleashing a high-pitched sound, opening its red eyes and shooting fireballs at Billy and Edison.

A zombie pigman walked past them, but Edison didn't make contact. He was too busy fighting the ghasts.

Two more ghasts joined the group, surrounding Billy and Edison with more fireballs.

"I can't do this anymore." Edison tried to catch his breath. "There's too many of them."

"We can do it." Billy shot an arrow, destroying one of the ghasts.

"We can?" A fireball nearly singed Edison's leg.

"The portal is just a few feet away," Billy reminded him as they shot arrows at the ghasts while trying to avoid the powerful blasts from the fireballs.

"I know," Edison said, "but it feels like we'll never get there." Another fireball landed by his feet. Edison jumped back and hoped they'd make it home.

2

FOUNDER'S DAY

"Use your fist," Billy instructed and punched the fireball, deflecting it and sending it back to the ghast.

"I won't get burnt?" asked Edison.

"No." Billy slammed his fist into another fireball.

Edison reluctantly made a fist and struck the fireball flying toward him. To his surprise, the fireball didn't burn his hand as he sent the fireball back at the ghast, destroying the white beast. He brushed his hand against his blue jeans. He couldn't believe it didn't feel any different than before. It was like magic.

"Let's go!" Billy called out as he raced toward the portal. "I think we have enough loot to trade in for emeralds and buy a map to the Roofed Forest Biome."

"That's awesome!" Edison said as he hopped in the portal. The two had been planning a trip to this new biome. Billy was doing a lot of research on treasures that could be found in a woodland mansion.

As purple mist enveloped them, Edison thought he saw someone in a green cape dash past, but when he went to take a second look, it was too late, and they had already spawned in the center of town.

"It's getting dark," Billy said as dusk was setting in. "I think we should head home."

"Yes," replied Edison. "I want to organize all of our loot so I can get up early and start brewing potions."

Edison and Billy walked toward their homes. They lived in a small seaside village called Farmers' Bay where they both had bungalows on the water. Farmer's Bay consisted of a cluster of beachside bungalows that shared a common farm. Everyone took turns working on the farm. As they walked past the farm, Edison saw Omar the Fisherman picking some carrots.

"Working late?" asked Edison.

Omar smiled. "I was at sea for a few days. I got a lot of fish. I was thinking of making a big dinner tomorrow night with the fish and these carrots. Would you guys like to join me for dinner?"

"That sounds like fun," said Billy.

Edison agreed. He was excited to have dinner with Omar. It was times like these that he really enjoyed living in the small community. There were always dinner invitations, and it felt like everyone was family. As he entered his house, he waved goodbye to Billy.

"Thanks for inviting me on the treasure hunt," Edison said with a smile.

"No problem," said Billy. "Don't forget to make some potions for me. I don't have too many left."

Edison got ready for bed, but before he retired for the night, he unloaded his treasures into a large chest in the corner of his room. He climbed into bed and thought about what a great time he had in the Nether. He fell asleep and woke when someone knocked on his door.

His neighbor Peyton was standing in front of the house, petting Edison's pet ocelot, Cranberry. She looked up. "Oh good, you're here. I wanted to see if you could make a meeting this afternoon."

"What's it for?" asked Edison.

"We're going to have a huge celebration for the Farmer's Bay Founder's Day. Omar got a bunch of fireworks and there is going to be a parade and a party. I'd love for you to join the committee and help us organize the event."

Peyton was always organizing celebrations. She had put together many memorable parties. Edison recalled one of her beach parties. It was filled with cakes and music, and at the end of the party everyone participated in a swimming race, which Edison was surprised he won. He wasn't the strongest swimmer, but the thrill of the competition invigorated him. He still had the ribbon from the contest displayed on his wall. With so many good memories from the previous parties, he wanted to be a part of Founder's Day. They had a small event to commemorate Founder's Day last year, but Edison knew it could be bigger.

"I'd be happy to help," he said. "I have a bunch of ideas that I wanted to share."

"Great!" exclaimed Peyton. "There's a meeting later today at the town hall. Can you make it?"

"I don't see why not," said Edison.

When Peyton left, Edison walked over to his brewing station. He had an entire section of the house where he brewed his many potions. He opened the chest, took out some Nether wart and blaze rods, and carefully measured out all of the ingredients he'd need to craft his potions. He was in the middle of brewing when there was another knock on his door.

Although Edison loved living in a small community, he'd admit there were also negative things about it. He was constantly being interrupted. Every time he started something, there seemed to be another person at his door asking him for help or inviting him to dinner.

Billy stood at the door. "Do you have my potions?"

"Not yet," explained Edison. "I didn't even have time to start them. Peyton showed up and asked me to be a part of the Founder's Day celebration meeting."

"I'm going to that too," said Billy. "It sounds like it's going to be a fun event."

"Well," Edison tried to sound polite as he said, "if I don't get any work done this morning, I'm not going to be able to make the meeting."

"I won't bother you," Billy replied and left Edison to spend the morning working on his potions.

Edison carefully placed glass bottles on his brewing stand and positioned all of the ingredients for a potion of Strength. He poured the water and added the Nether wart and the blaze powder and started brewing. He poured the batch of potion into several bottles. He was hoping to head into town later to trade the potions with the other villagers.

People traveled from across the Overworld to buy Edison's potions—he was a respected alchemist. Edison had a stand positioned between the library and the butcher's shop where he sold the potions. He loved making small talk with folks who purchased his potions and liked finding out how they planned to use them. He had one person who stocked up on potions of Fire Resistance because she planned on living in the Nether. After his trip to the Nether, he could never imagine living there. He had been so happy when he hopped on the portal to come home. He had gathered enough supplies from the trip that he wouldn't have to return for a while.

Edison began to brew his second batch of potions. As he organized all of the ingredients, he was startled by Billy rushing into his house. Edison was so surprised that he almost knocked over a bottle of potion.

"What's the matter?" Edison was annoyed. He wanted to work on his potions without interruptions, and he had already told Billy he needed to work.

"I'm sorry to barge in." Billy took a deep breath, and his eyes swelled with tears. Edison could see he was upset.

"Are you okay?" asked Edison. "Do you want a glass of water?"

Billy nodded as he spit out the words, "My treasure."

"What's wrong with your treasure?" asked Edison.

"It's missing!" Billy cried.

"Really?" asked Edison. "Are you sure you didn't just misplace it?"

"No." Billy was annoyed. "When I got back home, my front door was open, which I thought was odd. I saw a bunny in my living room, and I assumed that it just wandered into my house. As I looked around my home to see if anyone else was there, I spotted the chest I filled last night. It was open and someone had emptied it."

"Who would do that?" Edison was shocked. They lived in a very safe community. Yes, there were the typical attacks from mobs, and the occasional creeper had surprised many of them and treated them to an explosion, but nobody had ever had anything stolen from their home.

"I don't know," Billy said, "but I'm going to find out."

Edison looked at the clock. "We have the meeting at town hall now. Let's go over there and see if anyone can help us."

"How are they going to help us?" Billy paced the length of Edison's living room.

"Maybe someone saw something," suggested Edison.

As Edison and Billy walked to the meeting, Edison wondered if he should have hidden his treasure. He had left his treasure chest in the corner of his room.

Despite what happened to Billy, he trusted the people of the town and believed that Billy's treasure would be found soon. It had to be a misunderstanding.

3
STOLEN TREASURE

Omar and Peyton were discussing the fireworks celebration when Billy rushed into the room and announced, "I've been robbed."

"What are you talking about?" asked Peyton. "Nobody in this town would rob anyone."

"I thought the same thing," Billy clarified, "but my chest that was filled with all of my treasures from my trip to the Nether was emptied. I searched my house for the missing treasure, but it was nowhere to be found."

"Are you sure you didn't put it in another chest and it's in a closet somewhere?" asked Omar.

"No." Billy wiped the tears from his eyes. "I had everything in one chest and now it's all gone. I know it's hard to believe, but it's true."

As the group discussed what might have happened to Billy's treasure, his neighbor Erin walked in. "I can't seem to find any potions in my house."

"You were robbed too?" Billy asked.

"I guess so. I thought maybe I had misplaced them, because I hate to think something sinister could happen in our little town, but I can't find them anywhere."

"I had the same thing happen to me," said Billy as he told Erin about the missing treasure from the Nether.

"Wow, I guess my potions could have been stolen, but who would do something like that? We know everyone in town." Erin looked off in the distance as she spoke, as if she were looking at the townspeople standing in a line, trying to figure out which one would steal her potions.

Peyton wondered aloud who might be responsible for the missing items. "I did see a new person walking through the village. I tried to talk to her, but she wasn't very friendly. She walked into the library. I can talk to Liz the librarian and ask about her."

"What did she look like?" asked Billy.

Before Peyton could respond, there was a thunderous boom, and rain fell on the town hall, making the windows rattle. Peyton looked over at the door, which was being ripped from the hinges.

"Oh no!" Edison called out. "Zombies!"

The impromptu rainstorm had created a small zombie invasion. Three vacant-eyed zombies lumbered into the town hall. The gang wasn't prepared for battle—they were only prepared to discuss the fireworks celebration at Founder's Day—so they weren't wearing armor and they had to dig through their inventories for their swords. As the zombies lunged toward them, their undead rotting arms grasping at their warm bodies, the group scrambled to put on their armor and battle the smelly mobs.

Peyton was the first to grab her diamond sword, and she leapt at one the zombies with it, slicing into its rancid flesh. She struck the zombie two more times, plunging her sword into its stomach and ripping through its purple shirt. The zombie fell to the ground and was destroyed.

The others struggled to put on their armor while dodging strikes from the zombies. Billy wailed. "I've been struck by an arrow."

Arrows were flying through the gaping doorway where the door had been ripped from its hinges. Peyton slammed her sword into a zombie blocking the exit and raced outside, trying to see what was attacking them with a barrage of arrows.

"Skeletons!" she yelled. "There are lots of them in the distance. We have to be prepared. This is going to be a hard battle."

Edison wished the sun would come out and end this hostile mob invasion so he could spend his time figuring out who was behind the series of robberies, but wishing for the sun to come out wasn't a good plan. They were in the middle of a serious attack, and he had to come up with a real plan. He adjusted his armor and pulled out a few bottles of potions from his inventory. He splashed the zombies that crowded the entranceway. The skeleton's arrows weakened the zombies, making them easier to destroy with potions.

"Help!" Billy called as he ran out of the town hall and found himself cornered by three skeletons.

4

A STRANGER

Edison raced to his friend's side, dousing the bony beasts with a mixture of potions that annihilated the skeletons in seconds.

"Thanks," Billy exhaled.

"No problem," Edison replied breathlessly. He heard skeleton bones clanging behind him. He turned around and threw a potion at its bony body. Billy plunged his sword into the skeleton until it was destroyed. He picked up the dropped bones on the ground and handed a few to Edison.

"I hope nobody steals these," Billy said as he battled the remaining skeletons.

The residents of Farmer's Bay let out a collective sigh of relief when the sun came out.

Peyton, Erin, and Omar rushed toward Billy and Edison. They wanted potions and help in figuring out why there were robberies in the town.

"Do you have a potion of Regeneration?" Erin asked Edison.

Edison pulled a bottle out from his inventory. Erin thanked him and asked how much it would cost. Edison smiled. "It's free. Don't worry about it."

Omar fixed the door as the group walked back into the building to discuss the recent robberies.

"I can't believe we had this meeting to talk about the Founder's Day celebration and now it has turned into a much more serious meeting," Peyton said.

Omar finished the door and joined the rest of the group. He was a fisherman and also a skilled builder. He was always repairing doorways and replacing windows for the town when they were attacked by hostile mobs. Since he was an expert builder, he had the nicest house in town. While everyone else had small bungalows, Omar lived in a stone mansion on his own private beach. He generously lent the house to the townspeople whenever they had an event. The Founder's Day party was being held on his beach.

"Thanks for repairing the door, Omar," Peyton said, and the others gave him a nod.

"What is going on in this town?" Omar questioned. "For the first time in my life, I'm actually nervous that the treasures and other resources I have stored in my home might be missing when I return."

"I feel the same way," said Peyton, and she suggested they halt the meeting so they could see whether there were any more robberies amongst the residents.

"Before we go, didn't you say something about a stranger who was in the town?" asked Billy.

"Yes," she said. "I saw someone enter the library. I'm pretty sure it was a woman."

"Let's go talk to Liz the Librarian and see if we can figure out who that person is and why she's here," said Billy.

"She might be here because she wants to purchase potions," suggested Edison.

"Or she might be here because she wants to rob us," said Peyton.

"Let's not jump to any conclusions," said Erin.

Omar added, "We should at least talk to her."

They all agreed, and the group made its way to the library. Edison was sad that they had to question the stranger who visited their town. In the past, all of the residents of Farmer's Bay were always welcoming to strangers. Now he felt as if this newcomer, who might possibly be visiting the town to purchase potions from him, was going to be interrogated by them.

"I don't think we should assume this person is the one who is robbing us," Edison told the group.

Peyton reassured him. "Don't worry, we aren't going to attack her. We're just going to politely ask her a few questions, right guys?"

The group headed into town on a mission. Liz was standing in front of the library when Peyton approached her. "Hi, Liz. Is there someone from out of town who's in the library?"

"There was a woman with red hair and glasses earlier today, but she left a while ago."

"Did you happen to talk to her?" asked Billy.

"No," Liz asked. "Why? Is there something I should know about her?"

Billy explained. "Someone stole my treasures I got in the Nether."

Erin interrupted, "And somebody stole my potions."

"That's awful." Liz sympathized with them, but she also wondered if somebody might have stolen books from the library. She hadn't checked the shelves thoroughly in a while. She excused herself and went into the library.

Walking back to the homes, Billy asked Peyton, "Do you remember what the woman with red hair and glasses was wearing?"

"Yes," Peyton said. "There was something a bit different about the way she dressed."

"What do you mean?" questioned Edison.

"She wore jeans and a green shirt, but instead of a jacket, she was dressed in a green robe."

Edison stopped walking.

5

BREWING

"What's the matter, Edison? Are you okay?" asked Billy.

"When we were in the Nether, I saw someone in a green robe."

"Really?" asked Omar. "Did you talk to them?"

Billy was confused. "We didn't see anyone in the Nether. In fact, it was one of the few times that I've been able to obtain all the treasure from the Nether fortress. What are you talking about, Edison?"

"When we were on the portal, I thought I saw someone run past in a green robe. I went to take a second look, but it was too late—we were already in Farmer's Bay."

Billy was standing next to Edison on the portal, and he knew there wasn't anybody there.

"I didn't see anyone when we were on the portal and you never mentioned seeing someone there." Billy was certain there wasn't anyone in that section of the Nether. His years as a treasure hunter prepared him to always be on the lookout for people who might want to steal his treasure. In all of his years as a treasure hunter, nobody had ever plundered his loot; this was his badge of honor, and other treasure hunters respected him for it. Since he had never been robbed in the past, it made the stolen treasure from his house even more devastating.

"I saw it quickly. I went to take a second look and the figure was gone," Edison explained again.

"That would make sense," said Peyton. "I could see someone following you home and stealing your treasure."

"But what about me?" asked Erin. "I wasn't on the treasure hunt, so why would someone walk into my house and steal all of my potions?"

Omar reasoned, "Maybe they saw you leave your house and figured you must have some valuables there."

Farmer's Bay was a small and extremely safe town, which meant nobody locked their doors. This made it very easy for someone to break into people's homes and steal anything they had stored in their chests.

"I hope they left the town and this mess is all over," said Peyton. "I just want to get back to planning Founder's Day. I have a bunch of fireworks and I want to put on an elaborate show. I need time to plan."

"I love fireworks." Omar smiled. "I'd be happy to help you with the planning."

"Great," Peyton said as they reached her door. "Let's meet in the town hall tomorrow at the same time. We can start the meeting again."

"What about my treasure?" asked Billy. "Even if nobody else gets robbed, I still want to find my stolen treasure."

"And I want to find my potions," said Erin.

"We might not be able to find them. I'm sorry to tell you that, but it's true. I think the best idea is to acquire new treasure and potions," Peyton said rather coldly as she opened her door. Her pet wolf, Cookie, came out of her house. Cookie wagged his tail as he greeted her.

Peyton invited the group in for cake and milk. Billy didn't want to accept her invitation because she didn't seem to understand how much his missing treasure meant to him. He was doubly annoyed when he heard Edison say, "We'd love to come in for cake and milk."

This infuriated Billy. This wasn't the first time that Edison had accepted an invitation for both of them. Even though they were best friends, they were separate people. Edison had no right to say *we* would come in. Billy looked over at Edison, but he seemed oblivious to his glare.

When the gang entered Peyton's living room, she shrieked.

"Are you okay?" Omar rushed to her side.

"Look!" Peyton pointed at an open chest that sat in the corner of her living room. "It's gone!"

"What's gone?" asked Billy. He thought it was ironic that Peyton seemed so comfortable with his missing treasure, but when she was robbed, she became hysterical.

"The fireworks!" Peyton exclaimed as she raced around the house. Erin and Omar followed closely behind her. Billy and Edison were in the living room.

"We have to help her," said Edison.

"She didn't want to help me when my treasure was stolen," said an irritated Billy.

"Stop thinking about yourself," Edison told Billy.

"I'm not only thinking about myself. This was the treasure we were going to use to buy a map to the Roofed Forest Biome, remember? You wanted to join me on that trip."

"I know." Edison recalled their plans to go to the roofed forest. "If we were able to go we might find a chest of gunpowder in the woodland mansion and we could use that to craft fireworks to replace the stolen ones."

"But we can't go now, because we don't have enough emeralds to get to the map."

Peyton screamed from her bedroom, "Every one of them is empty. I have nothing!"

Billy and Edison joined the others in Peyton's bedroom. Billy said, "I'm sorry you've been robbed. I know how you feel. It's awful."

"We have to get to the bottom of this," exclaimed Erin.

Omar wondered aloud, "I hope all of my stuff is still in my house."

"Let's go check," suggested Peyton, and the group rushed out of her house and down the sandy path to Omar's home.

Omar's home was intact. "Looks like nothing was stolen."

"I hope the robberies are over and we were the only unfortunate ones," said Erin.

Billy and Edison excused themselves and walked back to their homes. Edison had a suggestion. "I have an idea how we can get the emeralds for the map to the roofed forest."

"How?" Billy asked.

"I can brew a bunch of potions and sell them tomorrow. I can ask people to pay me in emeralds."

"That's a great idea. Do you need any help brewing the potions?"

Edison nodded. "That would be great."

As they walked inside Edison's house, they were both nervous that Edison might have been robbed and they wouldn't be able to brew the potion. They collectively let out a sigh of relief when they saw all of the ingredients for the potions on the brewing stand along with the few potions Edison had crafted.

Edison carefully instructed his assistant Billy on what he needed to do as they brewed a potion of Invisibility. He pulled a fermented spider eye out from a chest. As he looked inside the chest, he noticed there were only two fermented spider eyes left when he was certain he had more than ten. In fact, the chest had been overflowing with fermented spider eyes that morning. He searched through the rest of his supplies to find that they had also been looted.

"Is something the matter?" asked Billy.

Edison didn't answer. He was too preoccupied with wondering why the thief only stole a portion of his supplies when they had emptied everyone else's chests. Did they think he wouldn't notice the missing supplies? He wished he could splash the Invisibility potion on his body and watch as he caught the criminal in action. The only problem was, they had no idea who was robbing them, and at this point the thief was an invisible threat.

6

ORIGINAL PLANS

"**A**re you sure the chest was full?" Billy asked.

"I'm certain." Edison looked through the rest of his supplies. "It's weird, but whoever robbed me just took a small amount from each chest."

"Maybe they did that because they didn't want you to know that you were robbed?"

"It doesn't make sense. They stole all of your treasure, and Erin's and Peyton's. Why would they only take a little bit of mine?"

Billy put a finger to his lips, signifying that they should be quiet. In a whisper he said, "Maybe they're still here?"

Edison quietly grabbed a sword from his inventory and tiptoed throughout his house. He searched every closet and behind every door, but there was nobody there.

"Perhaps they splashed themselves with the potion of Invisibility you had brewed when they heard us coming and then ran out?" Billy wondered where the thief was hiding.

"Or they ran out of room and couldn't carry it all," Edison said as he put his sword back in his inventory.

"What if they're still here and invisible?"

"They're?" Edison paused. "Do you think there are two of them? What about the woman in the green robe?"

"We have no idea if that woman is the one who robbed us," said Billy.

"But I saw her in the Nether," said Edison. "Don't you believe me?"

Billy nodded. "I guess so, but I really didn't see her."

"Okay, but what if the thief is someone from our town and they are just trying to distract us with the woman in the green robe?" suggested Edison.

"Do you think Peyton is behind this? She couldn't be, right? She is the town cheerleader."

"You're right. She couldn't be. Plus, she wouldn't rob herself."

"Unless she wanted it to look like she was a victim," said Billy.

The duo had many theories, but nothing could be proven.

Edison said, "I'm going to solve these crimes."

"Okay, but you promised me you'd go to the roofed forest with me. Can you solve this when we get back?"

"Billy, I have to do this now. You can't take a break when you're working on a case."

"Edison, you're not a detective. You're an alchemist. You don't even have any clues. Let's just go to the roofed forest like we planned, and then you can go back to playing detective."

"I have an idea. I can do both. I will set up my stand tomorrow, and I'll chat with all of the people who buy my potions. I'll see if there were robberies in neighboring towns. When I'm done, I should have enough emeralds for us to buy our map, and then we can plan the treasure hunt. I will also have more infor- mation to help us solve these crimes."

"You better not back out on this trip," Billy remarked as he got ready to leave. It was dusk, and he knew they would be vulnerable to hostile mobs.

As Billy opened the door, an arrow flew toward him, piercing his unarmored chest, and he lost a heart.

Edison quickly put on his armor and grabbed a handful of potions, but as he stepped outside, he wasn't prepared to see two spider jockeys on his lawn.

"Two!" Billy cried as he put on his armor. "That never happens."

Edison traded his sword for a bow and arrow and shielded himself as he stood in the doorway and shot at the skeleton, striking it with his first arrow. Edison was feeling good about striking the skeleton on the first try, but he lost his confidence when he stared into two sets of red eyes. The spiders, who were controlling the skeletons who rode atop them, advanced toward him. Billy struck one of the spiders with his diamond sword. He slammed the sword deep into the spider until the mob was annihilated.

"Good job!" Edison exclaimed as he unleashed a

wave of arrows at both skeletons. His arrows destroyed the skeleton that was displaced from the obliterated spider. Ten experience points dropped to the ground, but neither one of them could reach for the points because the remaining spider jockey was ready to battle.

As the spider jockey jerked toward them, the weakened skeleton fell forward and accidently hit himself with an arrow and was instantly destroyed. Billy raced over to the spider and slayed the arachnid in one swoop.

"That was intense," Billy sighed.

"You better get home quickly. We don't want to have any more battles," said Edison. He lit a torch and left it on the outside of his home to ward off any other creatures of the night.

Edison was glad to climb into bed at the end of the day. He pulled his red wool covers over his body and fell asleep. In the morning, he gathered all of his potions, placed them in his case, and walked toward the village. He knew he had to sell enough potions to get the emeralds for the map, but he was too busy focusing on the questions he'd ask the customers. He truly believed one of the customers would offer him some clues in solving this mystery.

7
CUSTOMERS

The sun was shining in Edison's eyes, and it made him squint. He was patiently waiting for customers, but there weren't any around. Normally he'd have a line of people wanting to purchase potions, but ever since he had gotten back from the treasure hunt, business was slow. He thought people must have believed he was still away. He never really left Farmer's Bay and had been worried that going on the treasure hunt might affect his business. He looked out at an empty street, hoping his business would pick up. There was a slight ocean breeze, but the heat from the sun was making him sweat. Edison was ready to pack up his potions when, suddenly, his first customer arrived.

A woman wearing a sparkly orange jumpsuit walked over to Edison's stand.

"Are you Edison the Alchemist?" She asked.

Edison recognized most of his customers, but she was new. "Yes, I am."

"Great." She smiled. "I need all of the potions of Fire Resistance that you have in stock."

"All of them?" asked Edison.

"Yes," she replied. "How many do you have?"

Edison looked through his supply. He realized he packed only two bottles of Fire Resistance potions. "I don't have much. I only have these two bottles." He pulled them from his case.

The woman sighed. "I guess that will do."

Edison wondered why she needed all of the potions, but he didn't want to appear nosy and just stuck to the basics. "Can you pay in emeralds?"

"Of course. How many?" The woman pulled a handful of emeralds from her inventory, which Edison found strange. Why didn't she wait until he mentioned how many he wanted?

"Two."

"That's a good deal. I wish you had more." She handed over the emeralds and he gave her the potions.

"I might have some more tomorrow," Edison said.

She began to walk away when he called out, "Where are you from?"

"Huh?" She turned around and walked back toward him.

"Where are you from? I haven't seen you before. How did you know I was here?"

"Everyone knows about you," she said. "You're famous."

Edison blushed. "I am?"

Before he had a chance to ask her more questions, a few regular customers appeared.

"Edison," one customer called out, "I'm so glad you're back. I need potions of Healing and Invisibility." It was James. James always bought Edison's potions. He lived in a snowy biome, and it would take him two days to get to Farmer's Bay. James always wore a heavy coat, and Edison wondered how he could keep it on during this heat wave. Edison was wearing a red t-shirt and jeans and was overheated.

Edison grabbed James's potions and handed them to him as the woman in the sparkly orange jumpsuit walked out of the town. He wanted to call out to her, but he knew it was pointless because she couldn't hear him and he had a line of customers. Edison was questioning if he'd make a good detective. He wasn't getting any answers in the case that he had decided to take on.

"How's life going in the snowy biome?" asked Edison. "Have you built a bigger igloo like you told me you wanted to do?"

"Things are good," said James, "and I did build a bigger igloo. You have a good memory."

The next customer, Anna, was from the neighboring town, and Edison wanted to ask her if there were any robberies in her town. "How are things in Verdant Valley?" asked Edison.

"Not good." Anna explained that two homes had been robbed. "My neighbor had an entire chest looted."

"That is happening here too!" exclaimed Edison. "I'm trying to help figure out who is robbing everyone."

"Wow, you're the town's detective?" Anna asked.

"Amateur one." He chuckled. "And I'm not getting very far in the investigation."

"I've also been trying to solve the crimes," Anna confessed, "but it's harder than I thought. We should pool our information."

"I don't have any information. We had stranger in the town who wore a green robe, but that's about it," said Edison.

Anna moved over to the side so Edison could handle the other customers. He wanted to question each person, but Anna distracted him. He felt as if she was questioning him. She asked him all sorts of questions about the robberies in his town, and offered very little information about the ones in her town.

"I have to go," Anna said and added, "When you get more information, let me know."

"Same with you," said Edison, but Anna just walked away without a reply.

Edison took note of Anna's behavior. He tried to question the rest of the customers, but nobody had any new info.

There was a long break between customers, and Edison was ready to pack up his wares for the night when an old man with long hair and a cane walked slowly toward him and called out weakly, "Are you packing up? Please wait."

"No rush," Edison replied. "Take your time. I'll wait."

When the old man finally reached Edison he said,

"I need a potion of Strength. My bones are so weak, and I'm so tired."

Edison looked through his case. "You're in luck. We have a bunch of potions."

"I need three bottles," said the old man as he readjusted his cane.

"That's three emeralds."

"I don't have anything to trade," explained the old man.

"I'm afraid I can't sell you the potions then." Edison felt bad for telling the older man that he couldn't sell him potions.

"I can barter."

"Barter?" Edison was confused.

"I will tell you your future if you give me the three bottles of potion," explained the man.

"My future?"

"I can see into the future."

"Really?" Edison questioned. He also wondered if this man was wise and could figure out who was behind these robberies, but he realized that he probably wasn't a psychic or someone who could predict your future, but rather someone who tried to get potions for free.

"Yes, really," said the old man. "You don't believe me?"

"No," Edison said, "I don't."

"I will tell you something about yourself, and you can tell me if you want to barter."

"Okay, tell me."

The old man looked into Edison's dark brown eyes. "You have a very good friend and he wants you to join him on a trip. You're conflicted because you don't know if you should go."

Edison was stunned. "Okay, we can barter." He handed the three bottles of potion to the old man, who quickly placed them in his inventory.

"You must go on this trip with him."

"But I'm not even sure we have enough emeralds to get the map."

The old man cleared his throat. "You do."

"Okay," said Edison. "What else?"

"I can tell you are very upset about something that is disrupting the peace in your town. You will find answers on the trip. Deep underground."

"What?"

"It will make sense when you find it," said the man, "but you can't give up. Even when it seems like all you reach are dead ends, you must move forward."

Edison found this reading of his future to be extremely vague, and it didn't make any sense.

"The only way you can succeed is through friendship," the old man said and walked away.

As the old man disappeared down the path, Billy came running down the street.

"Edison," Billy spoke quickly, "I found a cartographer and he has a map to the Roofed Forest Biome that he claims contains a woodland mansion."

"How much does the map cost?"

"Twelve emeralds."

Edison looked in his inventory. He had exactly twelve emeralds.

8

VERDANT VALLEY

"Great," Billy exclaimed, "the cartographer is in Verdant Valley. We have to meet him before dusk."

Edison wanted to tell Billy about the old man, but he wasn't quite sure how he'd explain the exchange. He worried Billy might think he was naïve for trading valuable potions for his fortune. Instead he mentioned what Anna had told him about Verdant Valley. "Anna bought some potions this morning and she told me there were some robberies in Verdant Valley."

"Really?" Billy was surprised.

"Yes," confirmed Edison. "We should stop by Anna's house and get some information about what is happening in her town. Like me, she is an amateur sleuth on the case."

Billy and Edison were on the outskirts of Farmer's Bay when Liz the Librarian called out to them. "Billy! Edison! I have something to tell you."

The duo turned around and walked to Liz. Edison asked, "What's the matter?"

Liz caught her breath. "I was curious if you had seen the woman in the green robe again."

Edison replied, "No, and I was in the center of the village all day. I was selling my potions. I'm sure I would have seen her."

"Why do you ask?" questioned Billy.

"A lot of books from the library are missing and when I was putting some books away, I heard two townspeople talking about how they were robbed." Liz spoke quickly. She was obviously upset.

"More robberies!" exclaimed Edison, and then he looked over at Billy. He wanted to tell him that they should find another time to go on the trip to the roofed forest, but then he remembered the old man's advice that he must go on the trip with his friend, and his even more cryptic message that he'd find the answers underground. However, he knew the logical decision was to stay in Farmer's Bay and figure out who was robbing the homes.

"Edison said there are robberies in Verdant Valley. We're on our way there. I will ask the librarian if books are missing from their library," Billy told Liz.

"That's a good idea," said Liz.

"I'm sorry, we'd love to talk more about this, but we have to go before dusk," Billy explained.

The duo ran from their sandy village toward the neighboring lush green biome of Verdant Valley. Edison was out of sorts from the change in biome. Thankfully both towns had great ways to keep cool in this heat wave: Farmer's Bay had a seaside breeze and Verdant Valley was shaded with large leafy trees.

"She's right over there." Billy pointed to a woman in a white robe. Like the librarian, the cartographer was also dressed in white.

The cartographer spotted Billy and walked toward him, "Perfect timing," she said as she looked up at the sky. "It's almost dusk."

"Twelve emeralds, right?" Billy confirmed.

"Yes." As they exchanged the map for the emeralds, the cartographer said, "You are getting an incredible map. I've been crafting maps for years and I must tell you this is a rare find. I promise that once you reach the roofed forest, you will find a woodland mansion."

"Incredible," Billy remarked. In all of his years as an explorer, he had never seen a woodland mansion, and it was his ultimate goal. He knew there were great treasures in these grand mansions, but he also feared the villagers, the hostile mobs that lived inside these mansions. He heard tales about the Vindicator from his fellow treasure hunter friends, and he was warned it was almost impossible to defeat. Yet, he didn't let these fears hold him back. As he clutched the map, he wore a big grin.

"Thank you," the cartographer said, and they parted ways.

The sky was getting dark and the absence of light meant that certain hostile mobs were already capable of spawning. Despite this fact, Edison wanted to make a quick trip to Anna's house to ask her about the robberies in her town.

"I don't think we have time to see the librarian," Billy said as he stared at the setting sun.

"I know, but we have to visit Anna before we head home."

"Now? Really? I want to go home and get ready for our treasure hunt tomorrow," Billy replied.

"It will be a quick visit. I promise." Edison bolted to Anna's house and Billy followed him.

Anna was surprised they were at her door. "Wow, it's so late. Aren't you guys worried about getting destroyed by a skeleton?"

"I just wanted to see if there were any more robberies here? We had a few more in our town," said Edison.

Billy added, "And Liz the Librarian said a bunch of books had been stolen. Has that happened here?"

"No." Anna looked down as she answered. Edison took note of this behavior. She always looked you in the eye when she spoke to you, so this was out of character for Anna. Ever since Edison proclaimed himself a detective, he searched for clues everywhere. "There is nothing happening here. It's all over."

"Thanks, and if you hear about anything happening, please let us know. Have a good night." Edison smiled, but Anna didn't notice because she was too busy staring at the ground.

"We leave town tomorrow and we won't be back for a while," Billy said, and Edison shot him a dirty look.

"Where are you going?" asked Anna.

Edison didn't want to give Anna any more information than necessary, and he was irritated that Billy was giving away their itinerary.

"We're going on a treasure hunt to the roofed forest."

Anna finally looked up. Her eyes sparkled. "The roofed forest?"

"Yes," Billy confirmed.

"How did you get a map to the roofed forest?"

Billy explained how he had met with the cartographer and how long he had been planning this trip. As Billy spoke, Edison stared at the darkening sky, worried they'd be attacked on the way home. He had his remaining potions in his inventory and didn't want them to drop to the ground if he was destroyed. He worked very hard to brew all of the potions.

"I've always dreamed about going to the Roofed Forest Biome," Anna confessed.

Edison's jaw dropped when Billy suggested, "Why don't you come with us?"

9
WHERE'S THE WHEAT?

Edison couldn't believe Billy invited Anna. At that moment, she was one of his major suspects. He didn't feel he could trust her. There were just too many signs that made him feel that she might be involved in the crime. She asked too many questions but gave no answers, and she couldn't look either of them in the eye. Yet Billy had kindly invited Anna on one the biggest and most exclusive treasure hunts in the Overworld. Billy didn't even know her very well. Edison leaned against the wall of Anna's home as Billy set up a meeting point for the treasure hunt.

"Tomorrow morning, we will all meet in front of your house. Okay, Anna?" Billy asked as he showed her the map.

"I can't believe that I'm going to see the Roofed Forest Biome tomorrow. I feel like the luckiest person in the Overworld."

Edison wanted to respond, *you are,* but he remembered the old man telling him the importance of friendship and he remained silent. Even on the walk home, when Edison yearned to raise his voice and ask Billy why he invited Anna, he didn't say anything. Instead he kept a close eye out for any hostile mobs and said good night before he jogged off to his house in the distance.

The next morning felt like it arrived in seconds. Edison jumped out of bed to find the sun shining. He had pulled an apple from his inventory and was taking a large bite when there was a knock on the door.

"Come in, Billy," Edison said as he wiped a piece of apple from his lips.

The door opened, but it wasn't Billy. Peyton was in tears. "I need your help."

"What's wrong?" asked Edison.

"There have been more robberies around town this morning." She sniffled and wiped tears from her eyes as she said, "Someone stole all of our wheat and the sheep from the farm."

"The farm?" Edison couldn't believe it. The shared farm provided all of the townspeople with food and wool—who would steal the sheep and the wheat? Edison rushed outside to the farm.

Most of the townspeople stood by the farm, staring at the field where the sheep lived, which was now emptied.

"Did you see the wheat is all gone?" asked Omar.

Billy sprinted over when he saw the crowd by the farm. "What happened?"

"Look!" Peyton pointed to the area where they housed the sheep. "Someone stole our sheep and the wheat!"

"It's amazing they were able to take so much, yet nobody heard them," said Erin.

Edison knew the person who was behind these robberies was quite skilled. He could assume this wasn't their first string of robberies. This made him think that maybe Anna wasn't behind the robberies. Perhaps there was someone else who was lurking between the neighborhoods and stealing all of their precious goods.

Billy was annoyed. Although he was upset they were robbed, he really didn't want to help his friends. He wanted to go on the treasure hunt of a lifetime. He had stayed up all night preparing for the trip. He studied the map for hours. This was the moment he had dreamed about for years, and now his trip was sidetracked because the town was in trouble. He knew he had to help out, but he was annoyed it would impact his plans.

"We have to find out who is behind all of this," Peyton suggested. "Maybe we can organize a committee."

Edison announced, "I've been doing some amateur sleuthing."

"Wow," Omar exclaimed. "That's fantastic news. Have you found out anything that would help us?"

"I know that Verdant Valley is dealing with some robberies. I don't think it's to the same extent as it is with our situation, but I have a friend there who is working on trying to solve the crimes in Verdant Valley."

"What else?" Peyton asked.

"I'm afraid that's all I have," Edison said softly. He was embarrassed he didn't have more information. He wanted to tell everyone about the old man, but he wasn't sure what the old man told him was true. He had to figure that out on his own.

Omar said, "I think we should all do some sleuthing. It's the only way we can solve this crime."

"I agree," Peyton said. "If we work together, we'll solve this much faster."

Even Edison agreed. He knew he wasn't a master detective, but he was learning, and he needed help.

Billy asked the group, "I know that we're in the middle of a major situation in town, but I was wondering if anyone would mind if I went on a treasure hunt with Edison."

"Now?" Peyton raised her arms in the air.

"I obtained a rare map to the Roofed Forest Biome. The cartographer claims that we will certainly find a woodland mansion. If we do, we will be able to get gunpowder, and Edison can make fireworks with it so we can have our celebration."

"That would be helpful, but I think it might be better if you were here," said Peyton.

Omar asked, "Why? They won't be gone long, right?"

"Hopefully the trip will be less than five days. That is, if everything goes according to the schedule I made," said Edison.

"I think that sounds fine. Why should you wait around here for something bad to happen?" asked Erin.

Edison and Billy said their goodbyes to the group. The townspeople wished them luck on their adventure. As the duo walked to Verdant Valley, Edison asked Billy questions about the trip.

"How long will it take to travel there?"

Billy took out the map. "I believe it will take two days."

Edison stared at the map. He could see the numerous biomes they'd be traveling through and took a deep breath; he knew this trip wouldn't be an easy one.

"Edison! Billy!" a high-pitched voice called out.

Edison looked up from the map and saw Anna rushing down their sandy street toward them.

"I thought we were going to pick you up from your house." Billy was confused.

"I've been robbed," she called out. Her eyes were swollen with tears. "I have nothing. I can't go with you."

"What happened?" asked Edison.

"Last night I put all of the items I'd need for the treasure hunt into a big chest beside my bed. It was filled with my best enchanted diamond sword, my diamond armor, potions . . ." Anna listed all of the items as she wiped the tears from her cheeks. "And when I woke up, it was empty."

Edison was shocked. "That's awful."

"Our town was also robbed last night. Someone took our sheep and all of the wheat from the Farmer's Bay farm," said Billy.

Edison realized that these crimes couldn't possibly be the work of one person. Nobody would be able to steal all of the sheep and wheat from their farm while also looting a chest in the neighboring town. There had to be at least two people behind these crimes. Yet he still had no leads.

10

A CLUE IN THE MINE

Billy suggested, "I have some extra armor and a diamond sword. Would you like to borrow it for the treasure hunt?"

"That would be fantastic." Anna smiled. "I didn't want to miss out on this treasure hunt because all of my stuff was looted."

Billy looked at Edison. "Do you have any potions or other supplies you could lend Anna? I bet if we pooled all of our belongings, we'd have enough for all of us."

Even though Anna was robbed, Edison didn't completely trust her, and he didn't want to lend her anything. Truthfully, he wanted Anna to go back home, and he was actually relieved when she had told them that she couldn't go. He didn't mention any of these thoughts, but replayed the words from the old man in his head.

The only way you can succeed is through friendship.

He pulled all of the extra items from his inventory and handed them to Anna.

"Thank you guys." Anna was beaming as she said, "If it weren't for the both of you, I'd never be able to go on this adventure."

Billy focused his attention to the map. "We have to walk through Verdant Valley and toward the hilly biome."

"Let's go!" Anna said as her inventory overflowed with items from Edison and Billy.

The trio walked through Verdant Valley. Edison wanted to stop by the library to see if any books had been stolen. He thought if he suggested it to Billy and Anna they would be annoyed, but he was surprised when he asked, "Can we make a quick side trip to the library?" and both replied, "Of course."

Edison walked down an aisle lined with books until he found the white-robed librarian standing by a shelf of books. He asked her if there had been any books stolen from the library.

"No," she replied. "Why do you ask?"

"The library in Farmer's Bay had books taken from the shelves and I know there have been similar issues with thievery in this town," said Edison.

The librarian had a blank expression. "I never heard of any robberies in our town."

A man dressed in a purple sweatshirt and jeans overheard the conversation. "Who was robbed?"

"I don't know," Edison replied. "My friend who

lives in the town told me about them. Last night, she had a chest emptied in the middle of night."

"Wow!" he exclaimed. "I have to ask around. Thanks for letting me know." The man called out to a woman who was standing further down the aisle and asked her if she had heard about the local robberies. She hadn't.

As Edison exited the library, he wondered if Anna had been making up stories about robberies in Verdant Valley. Could her story about having her chest emptied while she slept be a lie? He spotted Billy and Anna standing in front of the blacksmith's shop.

"Billy is so sweet. He got me a new pickaxe because mine was stolen and you guys didn't have an extra one." Anna showed off the new pickaxe.

Billy studied the map. "We have to get to the Hills Biome before midday if we want to stay on schedule."

Neither asked about Edison's trip to the library. He wanted to confront Anna and tell her that nobody had heard about the robberies, but again he remained silent. Although for the entirety of the walk to the hills, Edison wanted to take Billy aside and tell him what had happened.

"Look," Billy exclaimed as he raced over to a small opening on the side of a large hill. "I thought it looked like there might be an abandoned cave on the map, but I wasn't sure."

"Do we have time to mine?" asked Edison. "I know you have a very strict schedule."

"Don't be silly," said Anna. "There's always time to mine, right?"

Billy pulled out his mining equipment. "Yes."

"Now I can break in the new pickaxe." Anna clutched the pickaxe and adjusted her yellow helmet with her other hand.

Billy and Anna rushed into the cave without looking back for Edison. He followed them into the dark cave but didn't see his friends. Using the light from his torch to see in the musty cave, he still couldn't find anybody there.

"Billy? Anna?"

There was silence. As Edison walked further into the abandoned cave, two red eyes peered at him from the corner of the dark cave. Edison quickly traded his pickaxe in for a diamond sword and slammed the blade into the pesky spider, but the spider was stronger than he imagined. Edison jumped back as the spider crawled toward him.

"Watch out!" a voice called out.

Edison turned around to find two spiders crawling behind him. He was cornered.

Billy and Anna rushed to Edison's side. Anna pierced the weakened spider that was in front of Edison and Billy helped Edison obliterate the two spiders that crawled behind him.

"Thank you, guys," Edison said.

"We found a great place to mine," Billy told Edison.

"I'm convinced there's going to be a lot of diamonds there," said Anna as she raced down a dirt path in the dark cave.

Edison followed closely behind her and marveled

when he saw the large hole in the ground. It looked as if someone had started mining here and left before they grabbed all the loot. He knew Anna was right; this was the type of cave where you'd find diamonds.

"We have to start here." Anna banged her pickaxe into the blocky ground.

Edison and Billy joined Anna as they slowly broke away a layer of blocks to unearth the treasures that lay beneath it.

"I see blue!" Anna exclaimed.

Edison looked up as something caught his eye. "What's that?"

"I told you, it's blue. I bet we're going to find diamonds," said Anna.

"No, what's over there?" Edison walked over to a chest that was in the corner of the cave.

Anna and Billy followed Edison over to the corner. All three used their torches to see. The three torches provided enough light to see a line of chests.

Billy walked over to the first chest and looked in, "It's empty."

Anna and Edison looked through the next few chests.

"This one isn't!" Anna called out.

They looked inside the chest filled with diamonds and iron ingots sprinkled with Nether wart. "Oh my!" Billy exclaimed. "This my chest!"

Anna peeked in the remaining chests. "This one is filled with potions and this one has fireworks." She stopped at the final chest. "And this one is mine!"

Billy stood next to Anna. As he held his torch, he could see a door next to Anna's chest.

"Is that a stronghold?" asked Billy.

"There's only one way we could find out," Anna said as she opened the door.

11

I CAN'T SEE YOU

Anna slowly opened the door as Billy called out, "We can't just leave the looted treasure here. We should take it."

"No," said Edison. "We don't want the thief to know we were here."

"Stop trying to play detective, Edison. This is my stuff, and I want to take it back."

Anna agreed with Edison. "We have to surprise him. Just leave the treasure there," she said in a hushed whisper. "We will find the thief and capture him and then everyone can get their treasure back."

Billy didn't care about the plan. He wanted his diamonds and iron ingots back. He had been robbed and his treasure had been found, and he wasn't going to wait around until they captured the thief. This plan didn't make sense to him at all, and he decided to do what he wanted. He picked up the loot and placed it in his inventory.

"What are you doing? You can't do that!" Anna was furious.

Edison couldn't believe there was a period of time when he didn't trust Anna. He looked over at Billy in disbelief. "Put the items back," he instructed Billy.

"No," Billy said as he picked up the final iron ingot. "You guys are acting crazy. Truthfully, I don't care if the thief gets caught or not, I just want my stuff back. If you don't want me to carry them in my inventory because you're afraid I'll lose it again if I'm destroyed, I saw a llama outside and I can tame it and have it transport all of our stuff."

"That isn't why we don't want you to take your treasures back. We don't want to leave a sign for the thief," said Edison, although he felt like he was repeating himself.

"I don't care about the thief. I only care about getting my stuff back," Billy said a bit too loudly.

"That's awful," said Anna. "My stuff is also there, but you didn't see me take it. I want to solve this crime so it doesn't happen again."

Billy stood by the empty chest as Anna tried to reason with him. After a few minutes, he slowly placed his items back in the chest, but he wasn't happy about it. He wore a dour expression as he put all of the items into the chest.

"I wonder who is behind all of this," said Edison.

"I'm sure we'll find out soon." Anna opened the

door and walked into the stronghold. She barely made it inside the stronghold when there was a loud explosion. *Kaboom!*

"Are you okay?" Billy screamed.

"Creepers!" Edison called out.

"Anna!" Billy cried.

"I'm here," said Anna. "I was able to jump away from the creeper, but we have to be careful."

"Look down!" Edison warned them.

Silverfish crawled all over the dirt. The gang jabbed their diamond swords at the pesky insects, but there were so many of them, the act seemed pointless.

"Shh!" Edison put his finger to his lips.

The gang stood in silence as they heard voices from the other side of the stronghold.

"Does everyone have enough potions?" Edison asked as he readjusted his armor. Edison led them down the stairs and into a large library. The voices grew louder.

The trio walked toward the sound of the voices, but suddenly the voices stopped. They stood for a few moments, but there was only silence until Anna cried out in pain.

Billy turned around to see an arrow sticking out of Anna's unarmored arm.

"It hurts!" she wailed.

Edison pulled the arrow out of Anna's skin as Billy investigated where the arrow had come from. But there was nobody in sight.

"Behind you!" Edison warned his friend.

"Skeletons!" Anna could barely say the word as an army of armed skeletons marched through the narrow hallway.

The skeletons eyed the trio and unleashed an inescapable sea of arrows.

"We have to duck!" ordered Edison, but it was too late.

Edison awoke in his bed. Had they really found the treasure in the stronghold? He looked out the window, and it was light out. *Maybe it was all a dream,* he said to himself. Edison was brought back to reality when Billy raced inside his house.

"We have to find Anna and get back to the stronghold," Billy said as he took a sip from a bottle filled with a potion of Healing.

"Is she home?" he asked.

"I'm here." She stood in the doorway. "I TPed to you guys."

"We have to get back to the stronghold." Billy raced out the door.

Peyton walked down the sandy block between Billy's and Edison's homes and called to them, "You guys are back?"

"Yes," Billy blurted out, "and we found the fireworks."

"I know," she said.

"What?" Edison was confused.

"Someone returned them to the town," said Peyton. "They left all of the stolen goods in the town hall last night, and a few minutes ago someone told me all of the sheep have returned. The wheat is still missing though."

"That doesn't make sense," Billy said. "We found all of the stuff in a stronghold. It can't be."

"I don't understand either. How could you have all of the fireworks here when we found them in a stronghold in the hills?" asked Edison.

Peyton seemed irritated. "What are you guys talking about? I thought you were on a treasure hunt."

"We were, but we were destroyed by a skeleton army," said Edison.

"If you're not going on the treasure hunt, now that we have the fireworks back, we're going to have another meeting about Founder's Day this afternoon and you should come," said Peyton.

"We have to finish the treasure hunt," said Billy. "We haven't even begun."

"But first we have to go back to the stronghold," said Anna. "We have to see what's there. We weren't imagining it."

"I had the treasure in my inventory and I put it back," Billy said as he relived the moment in his mind.

Edison knew what they needed to do. He had no idea what they'd find in the stronghold, but he knew they had to go back there.

12

WITCH HUNT

Edison held his torch and stared at the wall of the cave.

"What's going on? Where are the chests?" Billy asked.

"Someone is trying to trick us," Anna said as she walked along the wall, searching for any clues that might lead to the person or people who had stored their stolen treasure in the cave.

"I wonder if they placed your treasure back in your house," mused Edison. "We should go back to Verdant Valley and see if it has been returned."

"We have to continue with the treasure hunt. I don't want someone to loot the woodland mansion before we get there." Billy stared at the map.

Edison tried to persuade Billy to pause the treasure hunt. "But we're so close to solving this case."

"Who named you the lead detective on the case?" Billy raised his voice. "Even Peyton and the rest of the town said it was fine for us to go. We don't have to be the first ones to solve it."

"Billy's right," said Anna. "I know how you feel, Edison. I wanted to be the star detective and solve the case. I wanted everyone in Verdant Valley to be proud of my sleuthing skills, but it's not about us solving the case, it's about the case getting solved. We made a promise to Billy. We said we'd go on this treasure hunt and we should stick to that promise."

Edison understood Anna's logic. He knew that everyone was trying to solve the case and he didn't need to be the big star that solved it first. He remembered the promise he had made to Billy. As he stared at the wall of the cave, his head spun with ideas of who might be behind these robberies, but he didn't tell his friends. Instead he muttered, "Yes, I think we should finish the treasure hunt."

Billy pointed to the map, "We have to get to the swamp very soon or we will be behind schedule."

The gang left the cave without exploring the stronghold, which disappointed Edison, but he knew he could return. However, he did stop in front of the cave. "Guys," Edison asked his friends, "if the case isn't solved by the time we get back from the treasure hunt, would you come back here with me and spend a day exploring the cave and the stronghold for clues?"

"Yes," Billy and Anna replied.

Anna added, "Of course. This cave will be our first stop. You have to understand, Edison, Billy and I want to solve the case just as much as you do, but you and I also made a commitment to Billy. This is a rare opportunity we can't pass up."

Edison did understand, he just didn't like the outcome. As they trekked toward the swamp, they walked through a forest dense with trees. The path was thick with leaves, and Edison could barely see his friends in front of him.

"Billy," Edison called out, "do you have shears? I didn't bring any and I want to clear a path for us."

"Good idea," Billy replied as he pulled shears from his inventory and ripped into the leaves, leaving a trail of fallen greenery on the dirt path. Billy paused, and Edison and Anna almost tripped over him.

"What's the matter?" asked Anna.

"I thought I saw someone in the distance, but I'm not sure."

"Really? What did they look like?" asked Edison.

"I think they were wearing a green robe, but it camouflaged them," Billy explained.

"Remember when I thought I saw someone in a green robe in the Nether?" asked Edison.

"Yes, and Peyton mentioned the woman in the green robe," said Billy.

"Are you sure this person was wearing a green robe?" Edison asked.

"Yes," Billy confirmed.

"That's a major clue," said Anna.

"But we can't get distracted." Edison couldn't believe he said these words.

"No, we can't," agreed Billy as he sliced through another layer of trees, revealing the sun's rays, which beat down on them.

The sun was almost setting when Anna called out, "I see the swamp."

Edison looked at the sky. "I don't think it's safe to keep traveling at dusk. We could get destroyed and have to start the trip all over again."

Anna stood by a path of grass near the murky swamp water. "Let's build a small house here."

Edison took out wooden planks from his inventory and placed them on the grassy patch. "I wish Omar were with us."

"Who is Omar?" Anna asked as she piled wooden planks atop the ones Edison had placed on the ground.

Billy replied, "Omar is a fisherman in our town, but he also builds these incredible homes. He has a mansion in Farmer's Bay, and he lets us have our town events at his home."

"Wow," Anna exclaimed. "That sounds amazing."

The group was working on a tight schedule: with each plank they placed on the ground, the sky began to grow darker.

Edison was placing the window in the house when he heard a noise in the distance.

"What's that?" shrieked Anna.

Boing! Boing! Boing! The noise grew louder until they were face to face with four slimes. Edison halted construction of the house and grabbed his diamond sword. The trio raced with their weapons toward the slimy creatures. Billy was the first of the group to cut into the icky slime, but he didn't destroy the bouncy beast. Instead the creature oozed and broke into smaller slimes. The gang slammed their swords into the smaller slimes and then began to attack the larger ones that cornered them by the side of the house. Edison used his free hand to pull a bottle of potion of Healing from his inventory. He took a sip, then passed the bottle along to his friends. With his newfound energy, he slayed the remaining slimes and helped finish the house.

"We can't forget to place a torch out front," Anna said as she picked out the last torch from her inventory and carefully placed it on the side of the home. As she entered the house, she heard an eerily haunting laugh echoing through the swampy night.

"Anna!" Billy cried from the doorway. "Watch out."

Anna turned around to see a witch laughing as it raced toward her clutching a bottle of potion. Anna froze as the witch doused her with a potion that left Anna with only one heart.

Edison handed Anna a bottle of milk, instructing her to drink it, as he lunged toward the witch, ready to defeat the swampy mob, but the witch was too quick to battle. The purpled-robed witch dropped a potion of Slowness on Edison and he felt as if he were walking in a trance. He was helpless.

Billy was the only one left to properly battle the

witch, and he nervously streaked toward it, piercing its hand with his diamond sword.

"Take this." Edison held a poisonous potion as he tried to call out, but his voice was weak.

Billy heard him and splashed the poison on the witch.

Anna screamed, "Take that, witch!" With renewed energy from the milk, she raced to the witch and destroyed the sinister mob in front of her hut.

"We have to get inside fast," ordered Billy.

The trio quickly returned to the house and crafted beds. As they climbed into their new beds, they wished each other a good night, but Edison wasn't ready for sleep. As he listened to Billy snore, Edison tossed and turned, and he couldn't get one minute of rest. He didn't want to have a bad night's sleep, so he did his best to relax. He thought about counting sheep. However, instead of counting sheep, he listed potential suspects in the case. He wanted to find the woman in the green robe. He was sure that once he tracked her down, he'd have answers. He was on his own personal witch hunt.

13
ARROWS

The morning was glorious and sunny, and the gang was excited when they studied the map and realized they were steps away from the Roofed Forest Biome.

"I can't believe we're going to finally see this biome!" Anna could barely contain her excitement.

"We should all drink this." Edison gave them each a bottle of potion that would help them increase their speed and they raced out the door.

Despite their ability to travel swiftly, the gang stopped when they spotted the oak trees and roofed leaves.

"There it is," said Billy in disbelief. "I've waited a long time to see this place."

"I heard that hostile mobs can spawn in the Roofed Forest Biome at all times because the leaves make it so dark," remarked Anna.

"Is that true?" Edison asked. He didn't know that much about the Roofed Forest Biome.

"Yes," replied Billy. He took out the map and said, "We don't need to spend too long in the biome. We just have to make our way to the center of the biome where the cartographer said there would be a woodland mansion."

This plan was one that was much easier said than done. Once the trio walked into the lush roofed forest, the beauty astounded them.

"This is a lot more verdant than Verdant Valley," Anna joked as she walked up grassy stairs that had red mushrooms sprouting on either side of the steps. She looked up at the trees that blocked the sky.

"I've never seen such dark and majestic oak trees." Edison looked and took in the beauty of the leaves.

Billy cried, "Ouch!"

"Are you okay?" asked Edison.

"I was struck by an arrow!" Billy yowled.

An arrow had struck his arm. The gang looked for a skeleton that might have spawned in the dimly lit biome, but there wasn't one bony beast lurking around the leaf-filled forest.

"That's strange," said Anna.

Before they could investigate, Billy called out, "I found the woodland mansion."

The cobblestone mansion was the largest house any of them had ever seen, and they marveled at the size and the detail of the home.

"I wish Omar could see this," said Edison. "He wouldn't believe something this grand actually exists."

Billy walked up the stairs to the entrance. Standing in front of the door, he looked up and couldn't see the top of the house. "I've read about these woodland mansions for a long time, but I could never imagine something being this awesome and stately. This is a home you'd only think exists in fairy tales."

"It looks like it could be a university building," said Anna, "not a house. I can't wait to go inside. Open the door, Billy."

Billy put his hand on the doorknob when he screamed, "Ouch!" as another arrow flew through the air and landed in Billy's shoulder.

Anna pulled the arrow out, and Edison gave him a bottle of milk to regain his health.

Edison looked for a skeleton, but again there was nothing there. They were in the roofed forest with no clues.

"There has to be someone trailing us," remarked Billy. He had been treasure hunting for years, and he knew what had just struck his shoulder. It was a warning shot. It was another treasure hunter telling him to stay away from his loot, but Billy wasn't going to give in. He had waited his entire life to explore a woodland mansion. He opened the door and the trio quickly closed the door behind them.

They walked through a grand foyer and into a room filled with flowerpots sprouting colorful flowers. "I've heard about these rooms," Anna said as she smelled a yellow oxeye daisy that was blooming in a pot.

"I want to find the room with a checkerboard floor.

I know there is usually treasure in that room," remarked Billy as he walked through the house with his diamond sword out. He knew they had to be prepared for a battle. The woodland mansion was home to three hostile mobs, but he wasn't that worried about the mobs that spawned in the house. He was concerned with the possibility of another treasure hunter shadowing them and waiting to rob them of all the treasure they would find.

14

MOBS IN THE MANSION

"I found the room," Edison called out, "but I don't see any treasure." Edison looked down at the checkerboard design on the floor and was certain he had discovered the room Billy had wanted to find.

Billy rushed into the room. "Look up," he instructed Edison.

Edison spotted the chest above the door, then he turned to watch Billy carefully pull out sticks and construct a ladder.

"Do you need help?" asked Edison.

"Yes." Billy smiled. "Do you have any sticks?"

Anna caught her breath as she ran down the hall toward Billy. "Edison found the room? That's amazing. Let me help you make a ladder. I can't wait to see what's in the chest."

The trio constructed a sturdy ladder, and Billy

climbed to the chest that was above the door. He opened it, "Guys! Diamonds!"

"Awesome!" exclaimed Anna.

Billy climbed down the ladder rungs and was splitting the loot with his friends when they heard a loud noise that sounded like a horn. They were enveloped with dark red smoke.

"What's happening?" Edison nervously asked.

"Look over there." Billy pointed at a gray creature dressed in a black robe. It was using its power to make a row of large fangs shoot up out of the ground in front of it.

"Oh no!" Anna tried to talk and hold her breath at the same time, which was an impossible feat. "It's an evoker."

The gang jumped back from the fangs, trying to avoid being destroyed by this strange creature. The smoke's color changed from dark red to white, and the evoker unleashed a piercing, high-pitched sound. Edison and the gang traded in their swords for their bow and arrows and shot at the dark, creepy mob that lurked in the cavernous mansion, but none of the arrows struck the mob before it dashed away.

The gang walked down the red carpeted hallway, and they kept a close eye out for any other mobs that might spawn in the poorly lit mansion. Edison said, "We should all carry torches." He looked at Anna. She was the only one who wasn't carrying a torch.

"I don't have any left. I used my last torch when we were in the swamp. I left it on the side of the house," she explained.

Edison and Billy were looking through their inventories for torches when a blue creature rushed past them and Anna cried out, "I can't see!"

The blue mob, which looked similar to a zombie, cast a spell of Blindness on Anna.

"That's the illusioner," Billy said.

"I know!" Anna was annoyed. "I want to see! Help me!"

Billy and Edison's jaws dropped when they watched the illusioner multiply in front of their eyes.

"One. Two. Three. Four," Billy said, "There are four new illusioners."

Anna shrieked. "Help me! I still can't see!"

One of the creatures, dressed in blue, grasped a bow and shot arrows at Anna. Billy and Edison lunged at the five illusioners, not knowing which was the original and which were simply illusions. Edison struck one illusioner, but nothing happened. Billy slammed his sword into another and quickly destroyed the remaining ones.

"You found the real one! Awesome!" Edison congratulated his friend.

Anna's eyesight slowly came back. She smiled at Billy. "I didn't get to watch you save the day."

Billy blushed. "There's no time for compliments. We have to loot this woodland mansion. This place is filled with mobs."

"Don't forget to pick up the bow the illusioner dropped." Anna pointed at the bow that lay on the ground.

"Thanks." He grabbed the weapon and placed it in his inventory.

Even with the light from the torches, the mansion was so dark that hostile mobs seemed to spawn in every corner. When two zombies lumbered toward them with outstretched arms, the gang used their swords to quickly annihilate the undead mobs walking in this mansion filled with treasure.

Anna raced ahead. "I think I found a secret room."

"What's so secret about it?" asked Edison.

Billy and Edison raced to the doorway and jumped back. The room was covered in cobwebs. In the center of the room was a spider spawner. Four red-eyed spiders crawled toward Billy and Edison. Billy swung at the spiders, swiping the side of one, just grazing the surface, but not causing any damage.

Anna was in the room, right near the spawner. "I'm going to deactivate it," she called out to her friends.

Billy wanted to warn her to be careful, but he was too busy battling the spiders surrounding him. From the corner of his eye, he could see Edison in a similar battle. Splashing potions with one hand and striking the spiders with their swords using the other, the duo skillfully obliterated the spiders while Anna deactivated the spawner.

"We're becoming experts at battling mobs," Anna said. She was proud of herself for single-handedly deactivating the spawner.

"I don't want to be a warrior," confessed Billy. "I just want to find treasure."

Edison remained silent. He had to admit that he was distracted. Although the beauty of the house enchanted him, he didn't really want to be on the treasure hunt. He wanted to be back in Farmer's Bay searching for clues and trying to solve the mystery. He paused when they walked past a room that contained only a large cat statue.

Anna laughed. "What is this?"

Billy looked in the neighboring room. "Oh my! This one has a chicken statue."

"This is the wackiest place I've ever been." Anna couldn't stop giggling.

"I know, these are bizarre rooms. One was filled with potted plants and these have large statues." Billy snorted when he laughed, which only made the group laugh harder.

Edison believed he struck the jackpot when he entered a room that was filled with chests. "Guys, come here! We just found treasure."

"Oh no!" Billy called out.

As Edison peered inside the chests, he found each one was empty. The room wasn't filled with treasure, but with a dark creature wearing turquoise pants and holding an iron axe. The beast swung its axe at Edison, but before the axe could rip into his arm, Anna and Billy's arrows destroyed it.

"What was that?" asked Edison.

"A vindicator," replied Billy as he picked up emeralds the vindicator dropped on the ground.

"Wow, that mob drops valuable loot," said Edison.

"I don't want to leave here with a couple of emeralds and some diamonds," explained Billy. "We could get that from selling potions and mining. I wanted us to come here and find real treasure."

"I agree. I think we spent about as much on the map as we earned on our trip here," said Edison.

"Now that we've battled all of the mobs that live here, we'll have a better chance of survival." Anna tried to see the silver lining.

"Guess so," said Billy as he held onto his diamond sword and walked down the hall in search of treasure.

"Look at this place," Anna called out. She stood in the center of a room with dark wooden archways. "It's really fancy, right?"

"A chest!" Billy sprang to a chest in the corner. He didn't pay attention to the detailed wooden archways and the craftsmanship. He was too busy opening the chest. "You'll be happy, Edison. Lots of gunpowder."

Edison joined Billy and gathered his allotted gunpowder. When they looked for Anna, they saw her jumping back from an axe that a vindicator swung at her.

"Help!" she cried.

Billy and Edison sped toward her but stopped when arrows cut into their arms.

"Ow!" Billy cried.

Edison tried to ignore the pain. He was focused on finding out who had shot the arrows.

15

DETECTIVE EDISON

Edison brushed the arrow off his body, racing toward the vindicator. He splashed a potion on the beast, hoping it would weaken him. The drops of potion startled the beast, and the gang sped down the hall, trying to escape the lethal vindicator. But the grey vindicator followed after them. Anna stopped and turned around, leaping at the beast with her diamond sword. It dropped emeralds as it was annihilated.

Billy refocused his energy on finding treasure. "There's got to be more treasure here."

Anna peeked into a room with two chests. They all walked inside the room and she opened one. "Awesome!" She pointed at the diamond chestplates that glistened inside it; the other chest was filled with redstone.

They emptied the chests and hurried to the next room, where they found chests filled with diamond hoes and gold ingots. Billy placed his last gold ingot into his inventory and remarked, "This is better than Christmas!"

"I know," remarked Anna. "We are finding treasure in each room. This is too good to be true."

Edison focused on the words *too good to be true*. He wondered if this was true. As he walked into the next room—which housed two chests, one filled with coal and the other with enchanted books—he remembered what the old man had told him. The old man said the only way he'd succeed was through friendship. He was with his friends, and he had an inventory filled with treasure. It didn't get much better than this. Edison smiled as they reached the next room. He wondered what treasure they'd uncover. What he didn't expect was to be struck by a barrage of arrows and to awaken in his bed in Farmer's Bay as the words *too good to be true* floated through his mind.

Edison looked out the window. The sun was setting, but he risked being attacked by a hostile mob as he raced to Billy's house.

"Billy." Edison opened the door, but it was empty. He wondered if he was the only one who was destroyed.

He decided to TP back to the woodland mansion when he heard Billy's voice.

"Edison," Billy called out.

"I'm here," said Edison. He raced to Billy's room.

Billy sat up in his bed. "I still have all the treasure in my inventory. Do you?"

Edison hadn't even checked, and he paused to see

what was left in his inventory. "Yes, I have all of the treasure."

"We have to find Anna," he said.

"But it's getting very dark." Edison stared out Billy's picture window, which looked out at the peaceful sea.

"I don't care. We have to find her," said Billy. "We can TP to her."

Edison agreed to TP to Anna's house, and they emerged in the center of her living room. Anna was pacing the length of the small room.

"Who attacked us?" Anna asked as she walked in circles around her living room.

"I didn't see anyone," said Billy.

"Me neither," added Edison.

"We have to find them," Anna said, as she banged into a chest on her floor.

"What's that?" asked Billy as looked in the chest.

"Oh my!" She paused and looked inside the chest. "This is all the stuff that was stolen from me. They must have returned it. I was so distracted trying to remember what I saw in the woodland mansion, I didn't even notice it."

Edison leaned down and saw the chest was brimming with all of the items Anna had told them were missing. He wondered who was stealing treasure and then returning it. It didn't make sense at all. He knew he had to crack this case.

"I think we should go back to the stronghold in the morning. It's the only way we can get answers," Edison said.

"I agree," Billy told him.

Edison was shocked. He thought Billy was going to suggest returning to the woodland mansion.

"I bet the person who attacked us in the woodland mansion is involved in all of these robberies," Anna theorized.

"But why are they returning all of the stuff they stole from us?" asked Edison. He had too many questions circulating in his head. He needed more answers, and he knew this was going to be another sleepless night as he listed potential suspects and their motives.

"Let's meet back here tomorrow morning and head to the stronghold," said Anna.

Edison was surprised that when he finally crawled into his comfy bed and tried to make a list of potential suspects, he had no suspects in mind. He focused on the person who attacked them in the woodland mansion. He replayed his last moments in the woodland mansion in his head, but he didn't see anybody when he reached the last room. He recalled the arrows that were shot at them as they explored the Roofed Forest Biome. Edison wondered if the person or people who shot the arrows had sprayed a potion of Invisibility on themselves, or if perhaps their clothing had camouflaged them in the greenery of the lush, leafy biome.

16

INVISIBLE

"Are you coming to the meeting?" Erin asked as Edison walked out of his house.

He was heading to Billy's house and wanted to get back to the stronghold. "I would love to, but I have to do something today. Let me know how I can help out."

"Did you hear the wheat was returned?"

Edison wasn't shocked. It seemed like all of the stolen goods were returned. "That's great."

"There haven't been any other robberies. I'm glad everything is back to normal," said Erin.

Even though there weren't any robberies, Edison thought things were far from normal. He wanted to solve the crime. "Yes, but they did take stuff from us. So I want to find out who was behind it. What happens if they try to do it again?"

"I hope you find them," Erin said and then asked, "Is that what you're doing today? Trying to solve the case?"

Edison smiled. "Hopefully."

"Edison," Billy called out his name as he hurried toward him. "Are you ready to go?" Billy was already dressed in his diamond armor and held his enchanted diamond sword.

"Wow, you're really going to battle," said Erin.

"Yes," Billy said. Then he excused himself to bolt toward Anna's house. Edison followed closely behind him.

"I'm ready," Anna said while placing her helmet on her head. "I'm also bringing a pickaxe. In case we have time to mine."

"This isn't a mining expedition," Billy reminded her.

Anna looked down at the chest in her living room. "If you guys want to take anything to replace what I borrowed, feel free." She looked through the chest, trying to find everything they needed for the trip to the stronghold.

"I think I'm fine, we have enough," Edison replied. Billy nodded his head in agreement.

The trio rushed toward the stronghold, passing two llamas in the Hills Biome. Anna asked, "Should we tame them?"

"Not now," Edison shouted. Even though the thief had returned all of the stolen goods, Edison felt a sense of urgency. He wanted to solve the crime quickly because he didn't trust the thief and feared they'd strike again, and the next time they wouldn't give back what they stole.

The three clutched their torches as they entered the dark cave. Two red eyes glared at them. Billy raced toward the cave spider and slammed his sword down, wiping it out with one strike.

"Impressive," Anna commended him.

Edison stared at the space where they had seen the chests. He was looking at the ground, searching for footprints, when Billy called out, "Look at the hole."

Anna and Edison shined their torches at the hole in the cave. Edison was shocked at how deep the hole was and said, "Someone must have done a serious mining job here."

"I bet they got lots of diamonds," said Anna.

"I wonder if there are any clues in the hole." Billy looked down, inspecting the blocky ground, but there was nothing.

Edison knew the only place they would find answers would be in the stronghold. As much as he hated being in a stronghold because it was dark and had many places where he could be trapped or imprisoned, he had to toss his fear of the stronghold aside and do a thorough search.

"We have to search the stronghold if we want any real answers," Edison announced, and his friends agreed with him.

Anna opened the door to the stronghold, and before they walked down the stairs, they heard voices again.

Edison whispered, "We have to be very quiet so we can follow the sounds of the voices. I also think it's a good idea to sprinkle the potion of Invisibility on us."

"But how we will see each other?" asked Anna.

"Let's splash ourselves when we get closer to the sound of the voices," suggested Edison.

As they walked through the dark and musty stronghold, Edison held his breath—the air smelled like mold and old gym socks. Every so often, he'd take a breath and the smell would overwhelm him. He wanted to puke.

"The voices are getting louder," said Billy. "Should we splash the potion on us?"

"Yes." Edison handed out the bottles, and the gang doused themselves.

"Okay." Anna's voice cracked. "We have to try to stay close together." She was worried they'd get separated in the stronghold.

At first Edison was nervous because they were all invisible and he feared he'd lose his friends in the dimly lit stronghold, but the nervousness turned to relief seconds later when the thief walked by them. Billy and Edison tried to silence their collective gasp as they saw a familiar face walking next to a woman wearing a green robe.

17

TOWN MEETING

The biggest problem with the potion of Invisibility is that it wears off. In this case, it wore off at exactly the wrong time. Edison, Billy, and Anna were visible to the potential thieves as the pair walked past them in the stronghold. They didn't have time to drink another sip. Edison put the blame on himself for brewing a weak batch. They were caught, but so was the suspected criminal.

"Edison and Billy. What are you doing here?" Peyton's voice had a casual tone, as if she had just run into them picking wheat at the Farmer's Bay farm.

"We could ask you the same question," Edison said.

"I was here mining, and my friend Allie and I found the stronghold," Peyton explained. "We were gathering items for the town meeting."

"I'm Allie," the woman in the green robe said with a smile.

"You were following us in the Nether." Edison took out his diamond sword and held it against Allie's chest.

"What are you talking about?" asked Allie.

"Leave her alone," Peyton hollered.

"I saw you. You must have followed us back and stolen the treasure." Edison inched the sword closer to her unarmored body.

Billy looked at Peyton, "You said you didn't know the woman in the green robe. You told us she was a stranger and a potential suspect."

Anna stood silently. She was confused. She didn't know Peyton, and she had heard about Allie, the woman in the green robe, but she wasn't sure why the woman was stealing from them.

Allie was annoyed. "You told them about me? You tried to frame me?"

"N-no," Peyton stuttered.

"Peyton, we know you're behind these crimes," declared Edison.

"How? Prove it," Peyton said. "I'm always the one putting together every celebration. I love Farmer's Bay. Why would I rob my friends? Why would I rob myself?"

Edison thought about the words the old man had said: *The only way you can succeed is through friendship.* The old man with the cane had said he'd figure everything out underground, and here they were underground. He also realized that the friends he was talking about must have been Peyton and Allie. The two weren't working together anymore. He wondered if Peyton telling them about the woman in the green robe was some way to ask them for help.

Edison said, "I don't think you're behind these robberies. I bet you're the one who convinced Allie to give everything back."

Peyton wiped tears from her eyes. "I was," she said softly. She looked over at Allie. "Tell them what happened. Please be honest. These are my friends."

"I thought I was your best friend," said Allie.

"If you were truly my best friend, you'd explain everything to Edison. He was working hard on this case, and he wants answers."

Allie confessed, "I am a treasure hunter, and I emptied my inventory on my last trip and I needed treasure badly. I was hoping to replenish my supply at the Nether fortress, but you guys beat me to it. I did see you in the Nether and I wanted your treasure. When I realized you lived in Farmer's Bay, I went to visit my old friend Peyton. When everyone was asleep I took your treasure, and I needed potions, so I took Erin's. I took whatever I could because I had nothing."

"That's no reason to steal," said Anna, and she added, "And then you came to Verdant Valley and stole from us too."

Allie stared at the floor. She sniffled. "I ran away to the next town and I noticed that people left their doors open and I just took stuff."

"I didn't leave my door open." Anna was annoyed.

"I saw you talking to the treasure hunters, so I assumed you had loot in your house. I went into your house and took whatever you had in the chest. But you have to remember, I gave everything back."

Peyton interrupted, "That's when I found out and told you to give it back."

"I listened, didn't I? Don't I get credit for that?"

Anna raised her voice. "You followed us to the woodland mansion and destroyed us!"

Peyton said, "I came to the stronghold to get Allie to come to the town meeting and confess. Ever since the robberies have occurred, nobody feels safe anymore."

"I'll go to the meeting," said Allie.

The gang TPed to the town meeting, and they emerged as Omar was addressing the group.

Omar spit questions at them. "What happened? Is this the woman who robbed us?"

Edison said, "We will explain what happened and then the town can vote on what we should do."

Allie bit her nails. She was worried what the town would do to her. Edison explained what had happened, and Omar was shocked. He questioned Peyton: "You knew about this?"

"Yes, and I tried to handle it on my own, which I now know wasn't the right way. I wanted everyone to get their stuff back and I wanted my old friend to go back home."

"Your friend stole from us," said Erin.

Peyton knew what Erin and the others said was correct, but she was torn. She believed her plan had made sense, but she understood why it wasn't popular with the townspeople. Peyton stood in front of her neighbors and felt as guilty as her friend Allie. She just looked up at them and said, "I'm sorry."

18

FIREWORKS

Peyton was stunned when Edison said, "It's okay. It was a hard choice. We're all friends here, and there are times when we each have to make tough decisions for our friendships."

"How can I make it up to you?" questioned Peyton.

"You're going to put together the best fireworks show Farmer's Bay has ever seen," said Omar.

The residents of Farmer's Bay cheered.

"Really? You guys aren't upset with me?" said Peyton.

Allie stood silently. Edison asked her if she had anything to say, and she responded, "My best friend betrayed me. What can I say?"

"How about telling us you're sorry?" Erin was annoyed.

Peyton was angry. "I feel like you don't even care about what you've done."

"I gave it all back. I have no idea why you guys are making such a big deal about it." Allie rolled her eyes.

Omar asked if he could speak for the group when he said to Allie, "I think the best thing is for you to leave Farmer's Bay and to never return. You don't have any friends here, and if you did, you certainly don't know how to treat them."

Allie looked at Peyton. "I didn't think this would cause this much trouble."

"And?" Peyton asked. She felt she deserved an apology.

Allie only said, "Goodbye," as she left Town Hall.

Peyton stared at the box of fireworks on the table. Days before she couldn't wait to have a Founder's Day celebration, but now she didn't want to celebrate at all. Edison watched as Peyton stood next to the box crying. He didn't know what to say.

Anna walked over. "Did you know that Verdant Valley was discovered the same time as Farmer's Bay?"

"No," Peyton replied quietly.

"It was," Anna said, "but we've never had anyone in our town plan a celebration for it."

"I feel bad for you," Peyton said. "The celebration is a lot of fun."

"That's because we don't have anyone in the town that is as nice as you," said Anna. "Do you think you could plan a joint celebration for both towns?"

"You'd want me to do that?" Peyton was surprised.

The town cheered.

"I think we all want you to do that," said Anna.

A week later, on Founder's Day, all of the residents from Farmer's Bay and Verdant Valley got together for a large celebration. Edison made a new batch of fireworks with the gunpowder from the treasure hunt in the woodland mansion, and they used Farmer's Bay's supply of fireworks too. The fireworks show was one that could rival any in the Overworld.

The finale had a spiral of red and green fireworks, followed by pink and purple ones that were shaped like stars. Edison took in the show as he thought about the old man's prophecy.

The only way you can succeed is through friendship.

"Thanks for helping put this together," Edison said to Peyton as he watched the sky light up in purple and pink.

The End

READ ON FOR A SAMPLE OF
THE NEXT BOOK . . .

AN UNOFFICIAL
MINECRAFTER
MYSTERIES SERIES

#2

BENEATH
THE BLOCKS

An Unoffical Minecrafters Novel

WINTER MORGAN

National Bestselling Author of
The Quest for the Diamond Sword

1

GREAT NEWS

"That's amazing!" Edison exclaimed to Omar.

"What's so amazing?" Billy overheard them. They were standing at Edison's potion stand in the center of town.

"Omar is building a castle in Verdant Valley," Edison blurted out.

Billy didn't find this to be amazing news. "Oh no, you're leaving Farmer's Bay?" he asked.

"Just for a few months," Omar reassured Billy. "I won't be gone long, and you can visit me."

Edison reasoned, "He's only moving one town over. It's a quick trip. It will also give us an excuse to visit Anna."

Billy looked down at the ground when he spoke. "I know you're right, Edison." He looked at Omar.

"I want to apologize. I realize you told me something really great, and I immediately thought about myself."

"You don't need to apologize. I'm flattered that you care about me moving to Verdant Valley." Omar smiled.

"Tell us about the castle," Billy said. "Will you build a moat?"

"Yes." Omar described the castle in great detail as Billy and Edison listened attentively.

"What made you decide to do this?" asked Billy.

"I was asked to build it," Omar replied.

"By whom?" Edison questioned.

"It's a rather odd story, but a few days ago I went to the village to trade some of my wheat for emeralds, and I encountered a cloaked man named Dante."

"A cloaked man?" asked Edison.

"Yes, Dante wore an orange cloak, and he asked me if I knew who had built the mansion by the water. Dante told me that he was living on a boat and had seen the mansion from the water and was instantly drawn to the structure. I told him that it was my home, and he immediately offered me countless diamonds for the building. I was taken aback because nobody has ever offered me a large sum of diamonds for anything I have ever built. There was a part of me that wanted to sell my home and take the diamonds, but I remembered that I love my home and never want to sell it. I explained that the home wasn't for sale, but Dante wasn't happy with this news.

"I told him that I could build him a home, and he suggested that I craft a large castle. I agreed. I didn't hear from Dante for a few weeks, but yesterday he knocked on my door and told me that he acquired a bunch of land in Verdant Valley and asked if I was available to start constructing the castle. I told him I could start this week."

"So you aren't moving there?" asked Billy.

"Dante wants the castle built very quickly, so I'm afraid I will be staying in Verdant Valley until the project is complete," said Omar.

Edison wanted to tell his friends about the great news in his life. He had run out of ghast tears for his potions, and he traveled to the Nether on his own and was able to refill his supply of rare ghast tears. The trip wasn't easy, and there were many times when he thought he'd be obliterated by a ghast or a blaze, but he had made it home in one piece, and he was quite pleased with the outcome. However, this news seemed rather minor compared to Omar's.

"I have ghast tears," Edison told his friends, "so I have to go home and start finishing a bunch of potions I was unable to brew before."

"Wow," Omar remarked, "ghast tears are hard to get."

"Yes." Edison told them about the trip to the nether.

"Next time," Billy said, annoyed, "can you ask me to go with you? I heard about a great Nether fortress I want to loot."

Edison agreed he'd tell Billy about his next trip to the nether, but Omar interrupted as he looked up at the sky, "It's almost dusk. I have to get to Verdant Valley before night. I want to get an early start on Dante's castle. Anna said I could stay at her house tonight."

Omar turned around and waved as he left the town ready to start building Dante's castle.

Billy asked Edison if he needed help closing up for the night. Edison was a respected alchemist and sold his potions at a stand in the village in Farmer's Bay. People came to visit his stand from all across the Overworld. As they placed the final bottle of potion into the case, a woman with long dark hair and glasses called out, "Can you just wait one second?" She rushed over, and catching her breath she asked, "Do you have any more potions for breathing underwater?"

Edison looked through his inventory and found one bottle of the potion of Water Breathing. "Only have one. Do you want it?"

"Yes," she said, "I'm so glad you have even one. I'm not a very good alchemist, and I've been in dire need of this potion. How much does it cost?"

"One emerald." Edison held the potion as the woman picked an emerald from her inventory.

"Thank you," she said. "You have no idea how helpful this is to me."

"I don't mean to pry," said Edison, "but it's very late. Where are you from? How are you going to get home before dusk?"

The woman pointed to the sea. "I live on a boat. Don't you see it docked at the edge of town?"

Edison and Billy looked over at the beach and saw a large pirate ship in the water. Billy asked, "Wow! That's incredible. That's your boat?"

"Yes." She blushed. "I built it. I'm a huge fan of pirate stories, and I've always wanted to live on a pirate ship."

Edison said, "Me too. I love pirate ships."

"If you'd like to go on the boat, I am staying here overnight, and I'd be more than happy to give you a tour of the boat tomorrow."

"Can I come too?" asked Billy.

"Of course," she replied, and then she added, "I'm Amira."

Billy and Edison shook her hand as they introduced themselves. Amira smiled and excused herself. "I have to get back to the boat before nightfall."

The two friends also had to get home before night. They didn't want to fight off the hostile mobs that spawned in the darkness. As the two cleaned up and raced back to their bungalows, an arrow pierced Edison's unarmored shoulder.

"Ouch!" he called out.

Four skeletons aimed their arrows at them. Edison put down his case and pulled out potions and threw them at the bony beasts. Dousing the skeletons with potion weakened them, and Billy slayed the skeletons with his enchanted diamond sword. One by one, Billy destroyed the beasts, and they dropped bones and an arrow.

"We did it!" Edison smiled as he picked up one of the dropped bones. "Let's go home before anything else happens."

Kaboom!

"I think it might be too late," Billy said as he regained his balance after the explosion.

"What was that?" asked Edison.

Smoke billowed from the shoreline.

"Amira's boat!" they exclaimed in unison.

2

PIRATE SHIP

"**W**e have to help Amira!" instructed Edison. "We can't! It's nighttime—we have to wait until morning," said Billy. "If we leave now we're going to be incredibly vulnerable to hostile mobs. Besides, we don't really know Amira at all."

The night sky camouflaged the dark smoke. Edison stood in front of his bungalow, stared into the darkness, and said, "We have to go. There was an explosion in our town. We have to find out what happened, but I should leave my case in my house. If we get destroyed, I don't want to lose all of my potions."

Peyton and Erin raced out of their homes. Peyton asked, "What was the explosion?"

Erin held onto her torch as she looked toward the sea. "It sounded like it was coming from the shore."

"We think a ship exploded," said Billy.

"The pirate ship?" asked Peyton.

"We think so," said Billy.

Edison quickly placed the case of potions on the floor of his small living room, closed the door behind him, and hurried toward his friends when he spotted zombies lumbering in the darkness.

"Turn around!" Edison hollered.

"Oh no!" Billy cried when he felt a zombie grab his shoulder. He held his breath to avoid feeling sick from the odor of rotting flesh.

Peyton and Erin weren't dressed in armor, and the zombies pulled at their arms as all four friends tried to grab diamond swords from their inventories. Billy readjusted his armor and raced to the zombies. Edison sprinted after Billy. He clutched a bottle of potion in one hand and an enchanted diamond sword in the other, and as he ran he splashed the undead creatures with potion.

Erin fumbled with her diamond sword, accidently dropping it on the ground. She tried to fight the zombie that attacked her while she picked up the sword, but the zombie was too powerful. With each strike, her hearts depleted until she respawned in her bed.

Peyton swung her diamond sword at the zombie that destroyed Erin. Slamming the sword into the fetid-smelling beast, she annihilated the zombie. Another zombie lurked behind Peyton, but she swiftly battled the zombie until it was also destroyed.

"Peyton!" Erin emerged from her house with a replenished health bar. She was dressed in armor and ready to battle any undead mob that spawned in the thick of the night.

Edison and Billy were in the midst of their personal battle against three zombies. Both struck the smelly zombies with their diamond swords. When the final zombie was destroyed, Edison picked up the rotten flesh they dropped on the blocky ground and said, "We have to race to the shore."

They hurtled past the town farm, and a familiar voice called out in the distance, "Edison! Billy! Help me!"

"Amira!" Edison screamed.

"We're over here!" Billy called out.

Peyton asked, "Who is Amira?"

"She's the person who lives on the pirate ship," explained Billy. "We met her today when she bought a potion of Water Breathing from Edison."

Amira followed the sound of their voices and reached the farm. Tears streamed down her face. "It was awful." She could barely speak.

"I know you're upset, but you're going to have to take a deep breath," Billy said calmly.

Edison suggested everyone head to his house, where they could talk safely. "There are zombies spawning all over here. It will be easier to talk in my house."

The gang crowded in Edison's tiny living room, and Amira spoke, "I was about to go on my ship when it exploded. Who would do that to me? I am just an explorer, I'm not someone who loots others' treasures."

Edison asked, "I know you say that you're just an

explorer, but can you think of anybody who might be a suspect? We should have a list."

"Wow, you sound like a detective," Amira said as she paced the living room trying to come up with any potential suspects. "Are you one?"

"I'm not a detective," Edison replied.

"We did solve the mystery surrounding a string of robberies in town," said Billy. "Edison, our friend Anna, who lives in Verdant Valley, and I did it together. It wasn't easy, but we did it."

Peyton wanted to change the subject and remarked, "You did a good job with that, but we have to concentrate on Amira's pirate ship. I was admiring it earlier today. I can't believe somebody destroyed it."

"I've been traveling around in that boat for over a year. I've explored all of the shore towns."

"All by yourself?" asked Erin.

Amira paused before she replied, "Yes." Edison found the pause slightly suspicious and made a note of it.

"Wow, that sounds lonely," remarked Peyton.

"It's not." Amira brushed her dark hair from her face. "I don't mind being by myself. Some might call me a loner."

"Well, if you don't mind some company," said Edison, "you can stay here until you rebuild your boat."

"Thanks," Amira smiled, "That's so nice of you."

Edison wanted Amira to stay in his house so he could keep a close eye on her; there was something about Amira that he didn't trust. He recalled how she paused when he asked her if she was alone on the boat. He wondered if she was telling the truth. He was also a fan of pirate stories, but he knew that pirates weren't good people. Maybe Amira wasn't just a fan of pirates, but was also a lone pirate who traveled from port to port, plundering villages. At the moment, she was his only suspect. Perhaps she had blown up her own boat? There were many questions, and Edison wanted answers.

Peyton yawned. "I think I have to go back home. I need to sleep."

Erin said, "Me too. Let's all walk out together. It's safer if we stick together."

Billy, Peyton, and Erin walked into the dark night while Edison showed Amira her new room.

"I can't thank you enough for doing this for me," Amira said, and she climbed into bed.

Edison was too nervous to sleep. He hoped that Amira wouldn't rob him while he slept. After he finally closed his eyes, he awoke to the sound of thunder. He rushed to the window to see the rain pattering on the glass. It was morning and the ground was muddy, and he noticed footprints on the ground. The footprints belonged to a wild ocelot that raced around his property. He looked through his inventory for fish to tame the ocelot. Once he picked fish from his inventory, he opened the door and put his hand out for the feral ocelot. It raced into the dry doorway. Leaning over his hand, the ocelot smelled the fish and took its first bite. The wild ocelot transformed in a tamed cat, and

Edison invited this new pet into his home. The cat rubbed against Edison, and he spoke to the animal. "I think I'm going to call you Puddles, since I discovered you in a puddle."

Puddles explored his new home, peeking his head into Amira's room. Edison followed the ocelot and called out, "Amira, my new pet wants to say hi."

There was no reply. Edison looked in the room. The bed was made and the room was empty. Amira was gone.